D1269502

The Fortieth Stone

MENUCHA PUBLISHERS

The Fortieth Stone

Andrea Ramon Eller

Menucha Publishers, Inc.
© 2022 by Andrea Ramon Eller

Typeset and designed by Deena Weinberg
All rights reserved

ISBN 978-1-61465-841-2
Library of Congress Control Number: 2021947318

No part of this publication may be translated, reproduced, stored in a retrieval system, or transmitted in any form or by any means, electronic, mechanical, photocopying, recording, or otherwise, without prior permission in writing from both the copyright holder and the publisher.

Published and distributed by:
Menucha Publishers, Inc.
1235 38th Street
Brooklyn, NY 11218
Tel/Fax: 718-232-0856
www.menuchapublishers.com

Printed in Israel

Rock and egg images courtesy of Freepik.com

To my beloved mother,
**Mrs. Bernice (Breindel)
Sommerstein**, *a"h*,
in gratitude for her repeated words:
"You have a flair for writing,"
encouragement for me to write

To my husband,
Kalman Eller,
my partner, my inspiration,
and my best friend.

Contents

Chapter One: A Worrisome Day 1

Chapter Two: Who's Boss 11

Chapter Three: A Fork in the Road 19

Chapter Four: For a Few Kopecks 25

Chapter Five: Dimwits and Sheep 33

Chapter Six: A Lonely Kind of Poor 37

Chapter Seven: The Plan 47

Chapter Eight: The Games Begin 53

Chapter Nine: The Lottery 59

Chapter Ten: Family Feud 65

Chapter Eleven: Hashem Winks 71

Chapter Twelve: A Chanukah Miracle 83

Glossary 91

Acknowledgments 93

CHAPTER ONE

A Worrisome Day

Long, long ago, in a Jewish village in Russia, lived grown-up twins in side-by-side houses. Feivish and Yossi were as similar as two orange lentils. Both had carrot-orange hair, carrot-orange beards, and green eyes. Both were tall and thin. Even their trousers and shirts matched, worn and frayed in the same places. And

they thought alike. One needed only raise an eyebrow, squinch his lips, or simply look at the other to share a thought or private joke.

The twins were married to sisters, Feivish to Breindel and Yossi to Gittel. Each couple had an eight-year-old son.

One frosty Thursday morning in Kislev, Feivish and Yossi leaped out of their beds to the sounds of the *klopper*. It was how they woke up every day. The *klopper*'s job was to *klop* on everyone's windows in the little town, calling, "*Deverkhen!* Wake up! Time to praise Hashem!" That day he added, "Less than a week till Chanukah! Watch for miracles! Watch for miracles!"

The brothers weren't thinking about miracles. It was too cold. They stamped on their dirt floors and shivered as they washed with chilly well water. As usual, they lit their wood-burning stoves to heat the kitchens. Feivish set his blue cloth cap perfectly in place, and Yossi mashed his yellow cap onto his own.

The brothers met behind their old, run-down houses. They no longer noticed the doors and shutters that hung unevenly. They couldn't do anything about the spaces between wood beams that invited drafts inside as if they were old friends. They ignored the roof that covered both homes, but sagged in a wide *U* shape from winters of wet snow. Some said the houses leaned on each other like two drowsy old men keeping each other from falling over.

Just as they did every day, the men fed the animals they shared. Feivish dished up food for the two goats in their pen. Yossi flung seed and corn into the chicken coop where four hens huddled against the cold.

That morning, the goats were not hungry. The chickens barely pecked at their food.

"Strange," the brothers said at the same time.

"Maybe it's too cold for them to eat," said Yossi, bouncing on his heels and rubbing his arms up and down.

3

Feivish stroked the animals' backs. "*Essen!*" he murmured. "Eat, little goats." They shivered. "Well," he said, "they'll eat when..."

"...they get hungry enough," Yossi finished.

The brothers didn't wait to find out. Yossi grabbed his tallis and tefillin, and headed for the *beis midrash*, a one-room barely heated cabin.

Yossi checked for his brother as he opened the door. "Feivish?"

No Feivish.

Yossi ran back to move his brother along. "Hurry!" he said. "Come now — not tomorrow!"

"What? Oh-h-h yes. I was checking the fringes on my tallis."

After *shacharis*, cups of hot chicory, and comfortable hunks of their wives' brown bread, the two men settled down to learn Torah together. The *beis midrash*, with its blackened walls, earthen floor, and windowpanes of paper, waxed to keep out the

cold, soon pulsed with the sound of voices, often loud, as men learned in pairs.

Feivish and Yossi immersed themselves in the Gemara. Learning was as necessary to them as rain was to roses. They'd soon forget the cold.

They had already forgotten the animals.

That same frosty morning, Breindel sped to the *beis midrash*. Wrapped in a stringy woolen shawl, she stood on tiptoes (for she was quite short) and banged furiously on the windowsill. She could see only the tips of a blue cap and a yellow cap through the cloudy papered windows.

"Feivish!" said Yossi. "It's your wife! It must be something important."

Feivish met her outside.

"Ah-*choo*, ah-*choo*, ah-*choo*, ah-*choo*, ah-*choo*!" (When Breindel was excited, she would sneeze in sets of five.) "Come quickly, Feivish! And bring your brother! Something is wrong with the goats!"

She and Feivish hurried home while

Yossi packed up their talleisim and tefillin. He ran to catch up.

At home, the two goats were trembling with cold, even bundled under hay. Their bellies rested on their knobby, folded-up legs. Feivish and Yossi carried the animals inside and set them by Gittel's wood-burning stove. Breindel and Gittel covered them with blankets.

"The chickens are sick! The chickens are sick!" Cousins Zelig and Mottel rushed inside. Each eight-year-old held a lanky white hen struggling to hold up its head.

Feivish took the chickens, scooped them up with his right hand, and cradled them with his left. After a minute he said sadly, "Yossi, I hold here two former chickens."

Zelig pushed away his *pei'os*. "Papa?" he asked Feivish. "Is it possible the number of former chickens is four? The two we left behind weren't moving."

Just then the goats gave a weak "ba-a-a-a." Their chins sank to the dirt floor.

Yossi stood up and stretched his back. "Feivish, we now own two fewer goats... Meaning we have no goats at all!"

Mottel, Yossi's son, jerked at his own *pei'os*. "Tatty! Where will we get eggs to trade for food? And potatoes for latkes? It's almost Chanukah!"

"Mottel," his father said, "the potatoes we buried deep in the earth will not freeze.

The earth will keep them warm. With Hashem's help, we shall have mountains of latkes on Chanukah! As for the rest, Hashem will provide as He always has."

Zelig tugged on Feivish's shirt. "But Papa! Where will we get milk to drink? And to trade for flour?"

"My boy, with Hashem's help, we have always managed. He will help us again as long as we do our part. Oh yes. Oh-h-h yes. We must ask for His help."

The twin's eyes met, mirrors of worry.

Gittel, as tall as her sister was short, raised her long arms to the sky. *"Gam zu l'tovah.* All is for the good! We have enough potatoes and eggs and onions and oil for latkes. That is, I *think* we have enough... Breindel? Do we have enough potatoes and eggs and onions and oil for latkes?"

"Ah-*choo*, ah-*choo*, ah-*choo*, ah-*choo*, ah-*choo*!" sneezed tiny Breindel. She patted her nose delicately with a leaf she'd

set aside that morning for sneezes. "Yes, Gittel. We have enough."

Breindel waited. "Gittel?"

"What? Ah. You sneezed. Gesundheit."

Feivish and Yossi returned to the *beis midrash*, now empty. They sat in silence that cold, sunny afternoon.

CHAPTER TWO

Who's Boss

Had it been a normal day, the two men would have studied as a pair for hours. It would not have been unusual to hear Feivish exclaim, "My brother Yossi is a *gaon*! Oh yes. Oh-h-h yes. I always learn from him." Nor would it have been odd to hear Yossi say, "Feivish? A *talmid chacham* he is! Maybe one day I'll reach his level."

At other times, the two would argue as they searched for answers to the Gemara's questions. Feivish might protest Yossi's ideas with, "A *bulvan* you are — a blockhead! Oh yes. Oh-h-h yes. It's as clear as glass that the Gemara is saying..." Or Yossi might slap his head in frustration at Feivish's thinking: "Such an *am ha'aretz* — a numbskull are you! It's as plain as day that the Gemara means..."

It didn't matter. Everyone in the shtetl knew the twin brothers loved one another dearly. They argued only as they dug for the Gemara's gems.

After a morning of study, normally they would have returned home to sell eggs and goat milk to Jewish neighbors close by, and to non-Jewish neighbors farther away. Then they'd hasten back to the *beis midrash* to continue learning. After dinner with their families, it would be back to the *beis midrash*.

This was not a normal day.

The brothers began speaking at the same time. Yossi smiled and said, "You first, Feivish. You're the elder twin."

Feivish nodded as he rubbed his chin. "Yossi, Yossi. Oh-h-h yes. Everything has changed." He pushed back his shoulders slowly. "I have made up my mind. I will put aside learning with you. But only for the meantime." His eyes flooded and he wiped them with his palms.

Yossi's head snapped up in surprise.

With a brave, determined breath, Feivish continued. "I shall work during the day to feed our families and learn late at night, after work. '*Ein kemach, ein Torah*' —without food, there is no Torah. I must earn a wage. You, Yossi, will continue to learn Torah, day and night. Nothing is more important."

Yossi tried to speak, but Feivish said, "Sha. Listen." He rose and clasped his hands behind his back, his forehead as creased as a small plowed field. Pacing the *beis midrash*, he said, "Perhaps in the marketplace I can fix the wheels on sellers' wagons. Or repair harnesses for the merchants' horses and donkeys. When I have earned enough to buy goats and chickens..."

Yossi stood, excited. "Feivish! We have been thinking exactly the same thing! Of course — we're twins! But *I* will work; it is *my* duty. We will be like Yaakov's sons. Yissachar learned, while his younger brother Zevulun supported their families." He pounded the table with satisfaction. "And I

14

will lose nothing. He who supports Torah scholars and their families is as important as he who learns."

Feivish was still.

Now Yossi strode in long, lively steps, back and forth in the *beis midrash*. "Someone at the railway station is sure to take me on as a porter. I can lift passenger bags from the trains, or haul water and shovel coal for the engineers."

"Yossele, Yossele." Feivish used the affectionate name for his brother. "It is *I* who must work. I shall learn in the early-morning hours and late at night as best I can. It will be a great loss for me. But it's your duty to learn for us — and with more fire than ever before."

"But Feivish! The ten minutes of life you lived before I was born are not to be sneezed at — not to insult your wife, of course! Those minutes are priceless. You must learn, and it is I who must sneeze — I mean, work." He blushed.

"Yossi." Feivish's tone was gentle. "You *know* you must listen to me."

"No," Yossi replied. "As difficult as it will be, I will support us. You will easily find a *chavrusa*. But don't become too attached to him. Once I've purchased goats and chickens, I'll be back."

"Stop. Jewish tradition holds that the firstborn decides such questions..."

"Firstborn?" Yossi snapped his fingers. "By ten insignificant minutes!" He flexed the muscles in his arm. "Besides, I'm far stronger than you. You'd be useless working."

Feivish's face flushed. "Enough of this. I shall feed our families through work, and you will feed our souls by learning." He managed a small, teasing laugh. "Don't be a *vantz*."

Yossi's face spread pink, then purple. "A *vantz*? A bedbug you call me? Well then, you're a shlemiel!"

Feivish stared at his twin, speechless at

first. "I believe you meant that! Since when do you call me a...a shlemiel? You've always called me an *am ha'aretz*! Perhaps you're a *tipish*."

"An idiot, am I?" Yossi banged his fist on the rickety table so hard it rocked. "You've always called me a *bulvan*! Apologize!"

"I? *I? You* will apologize."

"I will not, *ol*-der *bro*-ther." Yossi stretched out the words, mocking Feivish.

"Yossi!" Feivish shouted. "If you don't apologize, I'll... I'll..."

"Yes? What?"

"I'll pull your beard and *make* you apologize!"

"Ha! Not before I pull yours!"

Each grabbed the other's beard — and pulled!

It was a sorry, sorry sight for grown-up loving brothers wanting to sacrifice something precious, one for the other.

CHAPTER THREE

A Fork in the Road

Meanwhile, three townsmen clustered beneath the windows of the *beis midrash* listening to what they thought was a typical Gemara disagreement between Feivish and Yossi.

"Who will you bet on this time?" said one man to the second.

"I don't know," the second man replied.

"The Gemara must have presented a difficult question."

"Question, shmeshtion!" interrupted the third. "I hear chairs tumbling and tables scraping. A person doesn't learn Torah by moving furniture. I believe they're fighting!"

They peered through the window.

The brothers, seeing three flattened noses against waxy windows, realized what a terrible situation they were in — and in public! Torah study made a mensch of a man, yet here was a *chillul Hashem*! They were ashamed.

The brothers released each other. They smoothed their beards, which now looked like orange straw brooms, bristles sticking out in every direction.

Feivish slapped his blue cap against his leg, dusting the air. "If we don't want the whole village knowing about this," he grumbled, "we'd better leave arm in arm, the way we always do. And we must ask Hashem, right away, to forgive us!"

"Again he tells me what to do," Yossi hissed through gritted teeth. He pulled his yellow cap low over his forehead. "Ho, ho, Feivish!" he said loudly enough for the small crowd outside to hear. "That was good fun, wasn't it? You must admit I'm stronger than you!"

"Ha, ha, Yossi!" Feivish wasn't laughing. "You may be stronger, but I have the brains. Oh yes. Oh-h-h yes!" The two exited the *beis midrash*, each with an arm slung hard over the other's shoulders. They wore tight smiles and angry eyes.

When they were far enough away from the *beis midrash*, their arms dropped.

"Enough, enough." Feivish's voice was a whisper broken by a sob. "How can it be that we, Torah menschen, have called one another shameful names and raised our hands against each other?" He held his cheeks as his head swayed from side to side. "Oy, oy, oy. Gott in Himmel, forgive us!"

21

Yossi ignored his brother and slapped his own head. "Think. I must *think*. Our families depend upon us for food and warmth. We have money to get by for a short while, but we'll need more soon enough. Chanukah is next week! Once we've used up our oil and eggs..."

"...flour for bread," said Feivish aloud to himself. "We'll need Chanukah gelt and dreidels for the boys, raisins and nuts for our wives..." He thumped his fist against his leg. "I'm going into town to find work. Surely Hashem will bring something my way before the day is out. We're in a month of miracles!" Feivish faced his brother. "You, Yossi. You *must* go back and learn."

"No, no, and no." Yossi *klopped* his foot three times. "*I* am going to the center of town, and it is *I* who will receive help from Hashem."

They tread the three miles to town in a rageful silence, except for the crackle of frozen leaves beneath their feet and the

clacking of stones one of them (mostly Yossi) would kick. Feivish, usually slow, kept up with his brother this time. The road split. The brothers split. Feivish headed to the town's center, keeping the woods on his right, and Yossi to the train station, woods on his left.

CHAPTER FOUR

For a Few Kopecks

I t was a Thursday, the busiest market day of the week. Feivish blinked as well-dressed businessmen scurried in and out of three-story buildings. He dodged peasants, servants, Jews, and non-Jews, all shopping in the outdoor marketplace. Customers haggled for everything from fish to figs while vendors hawked everything

from firewood to featherbeds. Babies bawled, children chased each other between fruit and vegetable carts. Dogs, cats, and birds wandered free throughout the plaza, searching for food that buyers had dropped.

Feivish hadn't been to the marketplace in years. The explosion of activity astonished him. He stared at the wagons, carriages, peddlers' carts, and the crush of people choking the square. The market was more zoo than market with horses, goats, geese, donkeys, ducks, and chickens clogging paths between vendors. And everywhere, wheels, hooves, and feet created a muck of thawed earth, melted ice, crushed leaves, and squashed vegetables.

Using great caution, he approached a peasant, a cutler sharpening knives on a rough, rotating wheel. The man's shoulders sat as widely spaced as an ox's. His beard sprouted from the middle of his cheeks and plunged like a black waterfall to the middle of his chest. A loose-fitting blouse and thick

leather vest didn't hide muscled arms, nor did his black boots hide feet twice as large as Feivish's.

Feivish forced himself to swallow through a throat as dry as chalk. "Sir?"

"What do you want, Jew?"

Feivish understood that Russian peasants weren't fond of their Jewish neighbors, yet he was taken aback at the word spit out as a curse.

"S-s-sir... I-I want nothing, sir. But the spokes of your wagon wheels are quite crooked. If you'd like, I could fix..."

The enormous bearded peddler seized Feivish's shirt and yanked him close, nose to nose. "Do I look like someone who cannot repair his own belongings? I can straighten those spokes with my teeth!"

"Oh! I'm sure... That is..."

"Bah!" The man threw Feivish down. "No Jew touches my things. Maybe fools don't mind a Jew touching his things. Go bother a fool!"

27

Feivish, still on the ground, backed away… into the direct line of a wild donkey charging through the square screaming, "Eee-yorr! Eee-yorr!"

He scrambled up, reached, and grabbed its halter. The donkey almost swung Feivish back to the ground, but Feivish kept his footing. Panting, he managed to utter soothing words and noises to the animal.

A crowd gathered. In a voice casual enough not to further frighten the donkey, Feivish told them to stay safely away. The donkey responded to Feivish's voice and touch and stopped screaming. When Feivish scratched behind its ears, the donkey gazed at him with adoring eyes. It sat, facing Feivish as close as it could in the middle of the square, and put its heavy head right on his shoulder.

The donkey's owner came running. "Give him to me! Here's a kopeck." The peddler threw Feivish a coin.

Yossi had not yet reached the railway station. Once his brother had disappeared from sight, Yossi had cut through snowy woods to the market. The younger twin hid behind the corner of a building. Yossi almost cried when he saw the peddler throw Feivish a kopeck, worth less than a penny.

He drew back and rushed to the railway station.

The station was tiny. A few brisk, bright travelers dashed for the only passenger car on a parked freight train, while two men, rumpled and grumpy, stepped down. They headed for the pile of luggage the train-men had tossed to the platform. "Porter? Baggage porter?" they called.

Yossi raced to help with their bags, but a wiry man in overalls snarled at him in a strange language and shoved him out of the way. The little man slung the luggage onto his back and followed the travelers.

Ah, of course, Yossi thought. *Station porters work here. I may not take their work.* He smacked his head for the second time that day. *Yossi! Be smart!* Aloud, he said, "Hashem, please send something that will pay!"

Immediately a peasant boy of seven or eight appeared. He staggered under two buckets of water hanging from a yoke

around his neck. Yossi offered his help.

"Yes, please! They're so heavy. And I'm so small, you see."

The boy set the yoke down, and Yossi hoisted it around his own neck without spilling a drop.

"Thanks, mister."

The boy pointed to the front of the train and Yossi hauled the water. Two kopecks for the boy came flying from the water tender's hand; the boy leaped and caught them. Two kopecks for Yossi came flying from the water tender's hand. The boy leaped and caught them, and raced away. Laughter bounced from the engineer to the conductor to the porters before Yossi knew what had happened.

The discouraged twin studied his surroundings. Perhaps the older workers pushing great wheelbarrows of coal to fuel the trains would share their work.

Once Feivish had released himself from the donkey's attentions, he shortcut through the woods to check on his brother. When he saw the boy steal Yossi's money, Feivish wanted to chase the little thief down. Feivish returned to the market only when Yossi had earned a few kopecks for pushing coal.

The clouded sun relaxed in its cold sky, and the brothers trudged homeward, separate and alone.

CHAPTER FIVE

Dimwits and Sheep

Did you find work?" Breindel asked Feivish.

"Yes." He spilled four coins onto the rickety kitchen table. "Three times as much would still mean nothing."

"What did you do today?" Zelig pulled at his father's sleeve.

"I won the kisses of a mule." Feivish's face was so stormy, Zelig didn't ask any more questions.

"Feivish, dear, four kopecks are not nothing," Breindel said. "They will buy food. And tomorrow will be better, with Hashem's help."

"From your mouth to His ear."

After a late supper of brown bread and a bit of goat cheese, Breindel said, "I did not see your brother come home with you. Where is he?"

Feivish concentrated on his empty plate. "I don't know. I only know that I must work to feed our families, and Yossi must learn. It's not his fault he's dimwitted enough to oppose his brother."

"Feivish! You have never said such a thing! How do you expect Hashem to hear our prayers if you spea...spea — ah-*choo*, ah-*choo*, ah-*choo*, ah-*choo*, ah-*choo*! — speak that way?"

She tapped at her nose with a leaf. And

waited. "Feivish?"

He looked up from his plate. "Oh. Gesundheit."

"Thank you."

"Tatty?" asked Mottel. "What did you and Uncle Feivish do today?"

"And where *is* he?" Gittel asked.

"I played hammer and nail with a little boy. I was the nail. I don't know where Feivish is. I do know that *I* must work to support our families, and he must learn Torah for us, day and night. In this matter he has the brains of a sheep, and I don't speak to sheep."

"Yossi!"

Gittel walked into the icy night. She raised her arms to Heaven. "Gott in Himmel! What has happened between

these brothers? Please return peace to our homes!" She paused. "Excuse me. While You're at it, could You please help me find my ladle? I seem to have misplaced it..."

That night, for the first time anyone could remember, the brothers did not learn Gemara together. Each learned by himself in his own home...and each suffered.

CHAPTER SIX

A Lonely Kind
of Poor

The next morning, Feivish arose before the *klopper klopped* on his window. It had rained throughout the night, leaving a world of slush and mud. He washed up, lit the stove, and slipped on a ragged coat held together with a piece of rope at the waist.

After *shacharis* and an hour of Torah learning, by himself, he slogged his way to town over sludgy paths and slippery leaves. With fisted hands in pockets and chin almost resting on his chest, he was the image of misery.

"I miss Yossi," Feivish said to himself. "I miss talking to him and learning with him. We haven't argued since we were little boys." He jut his chin forward. "But he is obligated to listen to me. No. I'll show him who's boss. *I* will earn a wage and *I* will save our Chanukah. Oh yes, I will. Oh-h-h yes."

By the time Feivish reached the marketplace, quiet on a Friday, he had a plan. Businesses and shops bordered the square. "I'll offer myself as an apprentice to a blacksmith. Or a glass cutter. Or a shoemaker. I'll learn a trade in no time."

Shoik, shoik, shoik. With each step, Feivish pulled his shoes from the mud. By the time he stepped onto slats of wood — a sidewalk in front of the shops — mud had

splattered his trousers up to the knees and to the waist of his coat.

Moving shadows in the first shop floated along walls in the dim room. *Where am I?* he wondered. When his eyes adjusted to the dark, he saw animal carcasses swinging from the ceiling. A man twice Feivish's age entered from a door at the back of the shop. He was clean-shaven, except for a walrus mustache. His apron was caked and stiff.

It's blood. I'm in a butcher shop. Maybe I can work here, Feivish thought.

"What do you want?" the man asked.

"I... I..."

"I haven't got all day. What is it?"

"Yes. Oh-h-h yes. I would like to be a shochet."

The butcher bunched his eyebrows. After a long moment pondering Feivish, he said, "Come with me."

Feivish followed him back through the door.

"The God of the Jews is good to you. This is Dudel, my shochet." A chunky man in his seventies with a curly gray beard nodded. "He shechts for the Jews, and I butcher for everyone else. But he's leaving next week. What's your name? Do you know how to shecht a cow?"

"I'm Feivish. I learn Gemara. Everything — even shechting — is in the Gemara."

"But have you ever... Oh, never mind. Dudel, show Mr. Gemara what to do."

Dudel explained the process. Feivish seemed to understand well enough, but Dudel shook his head. He whispered, "I saw you with the crazy donkey yesterday. You like animals, yes?"

"I suppose so. They seem to like me," Feivish admitted.

"Look," Dudel said. "The Gemara may have explained in words how to shecht an animal, but I don't think you..."

The butcher pulled on a rope, and a chute door rose. In staggered a small, skinny

black-and-white cow. Dudel showed Feivish how to hold the animal's chin up, just so. All was fine. But when Feivish saw Dudel's knife, he teetered on his feet.

"Wait." Feivish felt his cheeks drain of warmth as his normal freckly color faded. "Just one moment, please..." He wobbled. He swayed.

He woke up amid sawdust and blood, breathing in the stinging smell of ammonia from Dudel's revival kit.

"Get out!" the butcher roared. "You've wasted my time, and distracted Dudel. You could have ruined a kosher shecht!"

Gevalt! Feivish thought. *Imagine how losing two goats and four hens can turn a life upside down.*

That same morning, Yossi had ignored the *klopper*'s wake-up *klop*. He'd made it just in time for the last morning minyan. Afterward, as he plodded in the rain to the railway station, in a coat much too short, he thought, *Poor Feivish worked so hard yesterday, and for so little. How awful he must feel!*

But one might have thought it was Feivish the way he thrust out his chin and said, "No. I will not give in. Ten minutes older, ten minutes younger... Feh! He is *not* my boss."

A train pulled in carrying planks of wood fresh from a sawmill. The good scent filled the air and pleased Yossi. He surveyed the

station. "Horses, wagons, just sitting. No doubt they'll transport the lumber. But there are no men to load the wagons." He scaled the flatbed car, hoping to assist the fellow standing on the pile of planks.

"What do you think you're doing?" The clean-shaven young man stood, feet spaced wide apart and arms crossed.

"I'll help move your lumber for a wage."

"What are those strings hanging under your coat?"

Yossi swallowed. "Tzitzis."

"What?"

"Something Jewish men wear."

The lumberman sized him up. "A Jew. You can work, *Jew*, but first I want to see your worth. Get off this flatbed and pull a plank from the bottom of the pile."

So. He thinks Jews are weak, does he? Yossi climbed down and looked for a likely plank. He seized one, low enough to reach, and pulled. It didn't, wouldn't, couldn't move. He hopped back onto the flatbed and

shifted planks around with his feet until his was less weighted down. The foreman, looking on, said nothing.

Yossi leaped to the ground. He grasped the plank and strained until sweat poured from his forehead, his neck muscles bulged, and his teeth gnashed. Inch by inch, the plank yielded.

Six muscled men watched from a good distance away, but Yossi didn't notice. He gave one last yank...and half the planks came crashing down. Yossi jumped backward into the mud, barely avoiding being pounded. Meanwhile, the men slapped each other on the back and laughed until they cried. Yossi stood, white-faced, while the laborers picked up the fallen planks and loaded them onto carriages.

"Well, look who saved us a lot of labor!" said one.

"Get out of here before we use one of these on you," said another, picking up a short plank.

"Hey!" shouted the foreman. "I'll say this much: You have muscle — for a Jew!"

Yossi held his head up in an attempt to walk away with dignity despite the mud covering him from shoulder to shoe and a red, red face.

It was early afternoon when Feivish and Yossi started for home, separately, of course. The market had emptied, and the next train wasn't due until the following day. More importantly, Shabbos would arrive early. The brothers had made fifteen kopecks between them despite their misfortune, enough to purchase chicken, vegetables, and wine for Shabbos. Yet they felt poorer than ever. A lonely kind of poor.

And whose fault is that? Feivish thought. *Yossi's!*

"Feivish is to blame for all of this!" Yossi moaned.

For the first time since their sons were babies, their two families didn't share Shabbos meals. They didn't sing together, learn together, or discuss the parashah with their children. Shabbos, the most beautiful part of the week, was only half a Shabbos.

CHAPTER SEVEN

The Plan

As Breindel lay in bed hours after Shabbos had ended, she whispered, "Hashem, please help us set things right between our husbands. If it takes a miracle, that's what I'm asking for during this time of miracles." With a soft smile, she thought of her own secret miracle.

"Oh no!" She tried holding back. "Ah-*choo*,

ah-*choo*, ah-*choo*, ah-*choo*! Pardon me, please. I'm sorr...sorr... ah-*choo*!"

She used the leaf she'd set aside and dabbed at her nose, as politely as she could. She cocked her head, waited, nodded, and said, "Thank You."

Gittel also lay awake that night, too troubled to sleep. "Yossi has never said a bad word about his brother," she said. "Breindel and I must make things right, and quickly. Please, Hashem, help us. And make it in time for Chanukah." Her eyes misted. "As for my own miracle," she said, "thank You." She turned onto her side to sleep, then sprang up. "Oh, I forgot! Could You please help me find my potato grater? I was sure I left it next to the sink..."

The next day, neither Feivish nor Yossi worked. The market was always closed on Sundays, and far fewer trains were scheduled. Instead, the brothers went to the *beis midrash* — and sat on opposite sides of the room. Their eyes were empty, staring

into open Gemaras. The shtetl buzzed with questions: Why weren't the twins learning together? Where had they been for the past few days? No one approached them to ask, and the women of the village could not pry a word from Breindel or Gittel.

When cousins Zelig and Mottel returned from their Sunday session of school, Breindel was ready. "We're going to play a game. Would you like to help?"

"Yes!" they shouted.

"First, you must find stones." She sent them into the woods bordering their small piece of land. They were to find smooth, light stones about the size and shape of a Russian kopeck, but the weight of two.

The boys brought home about sixty of the right-sized stones. Breindel scrubbed them until they shone. She set them in a chipped clay bowl and handed the bowl to her sister.

"Gittel," Breindel said, "you are the artist. Pick one stone and paint the letter alef

49

on it, please. We will have a lottery, using forty of these stones. The brother who selects the alef will learn as usual, and the other will have to work."

"Brilliant!" Gittel clapped her hands. "But Breindel! Forty stones? Six or eight would work just as well!"

"Gittel, dear. How many days did Moshe Rabbeinu remain at the top of Har Sinai?"

"Forty days and forty nights. Three times he did this."

"And how many days did it rain when Noach lived in the ark?"

"Forty."

"Yes. And at what age does a man become wise?"

"Ah! Forty! An important number is this forty. And *you* are very wise, indeed."

"Ah-*choo*, ah-*choo*, ah-*choo*, ah-*choo*, ah-*choo*!" Breindel sneezed quietly. She blotted her nose with a leaf.

And waited.

"Gittel?"

"Oh. Gesundheit."

Gittel removed a bit of burned wood from the bottom of her stove. She ground it into a black powder and mixed it with grease from the stove grates. Next, using a slim stick, she wrote a tiny alef on one stone. When it dried, she dropped it into the bowl with the others.

Forty stones.

CHAPTER EIGHT

The Games Begin

Sitting in the *beis midrash* that day, each brother had a headache. Listless and lonesome, they returned to their homes and ate brown bread and hot soup, and drank tea.

Feivish finished his meal and bentshed, paying special attention to the words "*Lo lidei matnas basar vadam...* — Hashem,

please do not make us dependent upon the gifts of men..." He rose from the table and headed for his bed. Little Breindel, her shawl wrapped around her, grabbed his coat off a peg in the wall and led him out the back door.

"What are you doing, Breindel? My head aches..."

"Feivish. Sit down," she said. "Gittel and I have a plan that will settle this argument between you and your brother."

"But I don't want to settle..."

She pointed to the goat pen. "*Please* sit down."

"But it's so cold..."

Yet Feivish dragged himself to his wooden milking stool. He sat with a tired thump, as if he were 150 years old. Breindel shut her eyes instead of rolling them.

Gittel donned her shawl and approached her husband. "Yossi, put this on." She gave

him his coat and they went outside. "We will resolve this disagreement."

"I want to lie down with my headache, under blankets where it's warm. I think I have a fever. And you don't need to fuss over me as if I were a child."

"Oh, but I do!" Gittel set piercing eyes on him. "Sit there. You do *not* look like you have a fever."

Yossi sat on a tree stump and shivered, a little too much, perhaps.

A narrow, splintery bench separated the brothers. Feivish, his eyes darting everywhere but forward, rubbed his hands and blew on them for warmth. He leaned back and looked upward, as if searching the clouds for something he'd lost.

Yossi felt his forehead with the back of his hand to test for fever. He was disappointed. No fever. He leaned far forward, finding something fascinating to stare at: a worm wriggling in the dirt, perhaps.

"Blindfolds," Breindel ordered.

Zelig and Mottel tied rags over their fathers' eyes.

"What's this?" Feivish asked.

"Hush," Breindel said as she helped the boys with the blindfolds. "This should not take long."

"Just do as we say." Gittel wagged her finger at the blindfolded men.

"You aren't setting us in front of a firing squad, are you?" Yossi joked, and Feivish laughed with him. They caught themselves and returned to their sullen, sour moods.

Breindel placed the bowl of forty stones on the bench. "You will each draw from the bowl between you, one stone at a time."

"I have painted an alef on one stone," Gittel continued. "Whoever selects it will learn day and night, as usual. The other will work. He'll learn as much Torah as he can, whenever he can."

"At least *someone* has sense around here," said Feivish under his breath.

"Better catch some while you can," Yossi

shot back. "Well?" he asked before Feivish could respond. "Who draws the first stone?"

"Your brother, of course," responded Gittel. "The firstborn."

Yossi jumped as if stung by a bee. With a broad grin, Feivish stretched his legs and leaned backward. He leaned back at such a severe angle, he had to catch himself before landing on the ground.

Once the brothers were back in place, Breindel said, "Feivish, select a stone."

Feivish's hand flailed in the air before finding the bowl. He drew and gave the stone to his son.

"No alef," said Zelig.

Yossi drew next and Mottel said, "No alef."

Feivish's turn.

"Blank!" said Zelig.

Yossi picked another.

"Blank!" said Mottel.

Feivish, Yossi. Feivish, Yossi.

Blank, blank. Blank, blank.

Soon, only the thirty-ninth and fortieth stones remained. Breindel asked Gittel in a low voice, "Are you *sure* you marked one with an alef?"

"Breindel! Of course I did! I may be forgetful, but not *that* forgetful. That reminds me... I couldn't find my broom this morning. Did you borrow it?"

CHAPTER NINE

The Lottery

Feivish hesitated. "Let's draw the last stones at the same time."

Zelig and Mottel, enjoying the game, shouted, "One, two, three...draw!"

The brothers drew. Feivish gave his stone to Breindel, and Yossi gave his to Gittel.

Gittel glanced at her husband's stone. She held it up for all to see the alef, and sighed

with some relief. "My Yossi will learn, and Feivish will work," she said. "Imagine. All the way at the bottom! Well, it's done."

The brothers removed their blindfolds and shook hands, embarrassed at the tumult they had caused.

"Ah-*choo*, ah-*choo*, ah-*choo*, ah-*choo*, ah-*choo*!" Breindel sneezed almost violently. "Wait!"

"Gesundheit!" all said in unison.

"Oh. Thank y... No, not that! Look!" She held up Feivish's stone.

It was identical to Yossi's. A second alef.

No one spoke for a moment.

Gittel stood straight. "I... I... I..."

"Why did you mark two?" Breindel asked.

"I didn't! I mean, I'm sure I didn't mark two!"

"Well, it didn't fall from the sky, Gittel!"

"Oh dear. There were so many stones. I didn't intend... Oh, I suppose I must have marked two. I'm so sorry."

"Oy, Gittel." Breindel sighed.

"My wife made a simple mistake. These things happen."

"Frequently," Breindel murmured.

"Don't you worry, Gittel," said Yossi. "We'll do it again. But we'll use ten stones this time."

"No!" said Breindel. "Forty is important. We Jews spent forty years in the desert..."

"We don't have that much time, sister-in-law," said Yossi.

"My wife says forty, so forty it is," Feivish said, with a hard look at his brother. "Oh yes. Oh-h-h yes."

Zelig nudged Mottel. "We'll take one of the alefs and replace it with a blank. Right, Mottel?"

Mottel put one of the alefs in his pocket. The boys ran to Gittel's kitchen for a blank stone and ran back to add it to the other thirty-nine. Mottel stirred them thoroughly with a wooden spoon.

Forty stones.

The cousins blindfolded their fathers for the second lottery. It went quickly. Feivish — no alef. Yossi — no alef. Again and again, clean stones. Breindel held her nose to keep from sneezing, and Gittel folded her arms and tapped her toe in short, nervous taps. How likely was it that the alef stone would be last again?

Feivish and Yossi drew and drew from the clay bowl.

Two stones left.

"This...this...is out of the ordinary," said Feivish.

Zelig and Mottel traded confused looks.

"Papa," Zelig said, "perhaps it is not so strange? We learned this year about chances in math. Say there are forty things, any things, one on top of the other in a pile. The chance of any one thing being at the bottom is one in forty. The chances of the same thing being at the bottom twice in a row is forty squared, so that would be..."

"Forty times forty is forty squared...so that's one chance in one thousand six hundred tries!" Mottel yelled.

"No squares or circles or triangles!" Gittel stamped her foot. "Hashem is running this lottery. There is no such thing as chance."

"Let's draw together," Yossi said.

"One, two, three..."

Feivish and Yossi handed the stones to their wives.

"My Feivish has the alef," said Breindel. "He will learn."

The brothers unmasked themselves, and, still unable to look one another in the eye, shook hands.

Silently, Gittel raised one long arm and waved it over her head. The rest stared. Gittel opened her fist and displayed Yossi's stone.

Another alef.

CHAPTER TEN

Family Feud

E veryone spoke at once.

"Mottel! You were to take *away* a marked stone!"

"Are you playing tricks on us?"

"Oh, my head hurts. I'm cold."

"Mine hurts worse. And I have a fever."

Breindel was not happy. "Mottel. I want to see the alef stone — the second one — that

you put into your pocket."

Gittel's eyes shot sudden fire. "Are you accusing *my* Motti? Mottel, show her the alef stone."

Mottel hung his head. He put his hand in his pocket and pulled out...nothing. "We thought it would be funny to put the second alef stone back so there would be two again," he said.

Zelig spoke up quickly. "It's not Mottel's fault. I told him to do it. He listens to me because I'm older."

Feivish squinted at Zelig. "My son would do such a thing? Is that what you did for the first lottery as well?"

"No, Papa. We did nothing the first time. Not one thing. I'm telling you the truth. Just this lottery."

Gittel eyed her sister darkly. "So! Your Zelig is at fault!"

Breindel glowered at Gittel and pulled Zelig to her side. "You know full well that the one who commits the crime is most

responsible, not the one who plans it. That's what the Torah says. This is Mottel's doing!"

With hands behind his back, Mottel looked at his shoes. Zelig scuffed a wide half circle around himself in the half-frozen ground.

"But Mottel," said Yossi. "How did you put the alefs at the bottom of the bowl?"

"He didn't! Did you, Mottel?" Zelig said.

Mottel's eyes widened. "I didn't do anything like that, Tatty! Really, it happened by itself." He was almost crying.

This time, Breindel did roll her eyes.

"If my boy says he did nothing, he did nothing," said Gittel. "We all saw him stir up the stones with my wooden spoon." She whispered to Mottel, "Where in the world did you find my spoon?"

Yossi said, "It's not so strange that the stones were last. The boys said it *could* happen twice in a row."

"Could happen?" said Breindel, hands on hips. "Nothing just *happens*. This is *narishkeit*!"

"Don't speak to my husband that way, Breindel. Even though it *is* ridiculous."

The families stood on opposite sides of the bench glaring at each other.

"Stop!" Feivish broke the tension. "This *mishegas* has gone too far. Breindel, please keep the two alef stones in your apron. Sister-in-law, kindly select two clean stones — you have extras, correct? — and mark *one*. We shall watch."

"Feivish. *You* do not tell my wife what to do. *I* tell her." Yossi turned to Gittel. "Kindly pick two stones from the extras and mark only *one* of them with an alef. All of us will watch."

"Now where did I put..." Gittel wrung her hands on her way back to the house. But within a moment she returned with the homemade ink, the stick, and a blank stone. All watched as she drew an alef on it.

Breindel gathered the thirty-eight blank stones used twice before, and held each one up for all to inspect. She displayed a

thirty-ninth, blank as well, and added it to the pile.

"Do you want us to put in the alef and shake the bowl?" asked Zelig.

Mottel shouted, "Yes!" jumping up and down.

"*No!*" said four parents in unison.

"You may watch from a distance," said Gittel. "Stand next to the chicken coop." She raised the fortieth stone with its alef for all to see and dropped it into the bowl — *plunk*! She shook the bowl, hard.

This time, the wives adjusted the blind-folds on their husbands, and the third lottery began.

CHAPTER ELEVEN

Hashem Winks

F eivish and Yossi drew each stone with great caution.

Blank after blank.

Feivish felt around for his son and pulled him close. "Zelig, how likely is it that the alef would be last a third time?"

"Papa, it's possible, but unlikely. It would be one chance in...Mottel?"

"Once within sixty-four thousand tries," Mottel replied.

Gittel's face was pale. "Chance, shmance," she said. "Likely, shmikely! Would you deny that Hashem is in charge, here and now?"

"My wife is correct," said Yossi. "Hashem is conducting the lottery."

All fell silent.

Four stones left. Breindel and Gittel came nearer to watch, and the cousins crept close. All held their breaths.

Feivish — blank.

Yossi — blank.

Breindel said in a dry voice, "Gott in Himmel! Ah-*choo*, ah-*choo*, ah-*choo*, ah-*choo*, ah-*choo*!"

"Stop sneezing now! This instant!" said Gittel.

"Well!" Breindel straightened herself to her full four feet and ten inches. "It's not as if I sneeze on purpose..."

"Sha!" Feivish said. "It's my turn to draw a stone."

But Yossi had untied his own blindfold. He stood, eyes and nose wet and rosy red. "Feivish," he said. "Please take off your blindfold."

Feivish slowly did so.

Yossi's voice trembled. "I'm sorry for the things I said to you, and the way I behaved on the day we lost our animals. You're right. You are the older and wiser of us. More than that, you're my dearest friend!" He wiped his face and nose with his blindfold. "Please forgive me."

Feivish was standing, his blindfold around his neck. Blinking rapidly, he tried, and failed, to stop tears from seeping into his beard.

"Yossi, I was wrong," he said, his voice cracking, "to speak to you the way I did. Ten minutes older, ten minutes younger — it means nothing given the wonderful brother you are. Life is not as sweet without our friendship and love. Can you forgive me?"

The brothers hugged and patted one

another on the back, while Breindel and Gittel held hands and dabbed at their own eyes with their aprons. Zelig and Mottel didn't know where to look. Their parents were crying, and it wasn't even Yom Kippur!

Feivish and Yossi closed their eyes and drew for the last time, keeping their stones hidden in clenched fists. Two wives and two children stood on their toes to see what the brothers had drawn.

Feivish checked his hand, and closed it again. He peered at Yossi with an expression only his twin could decipher.

Yossi returned the look and nodded.

"They're communicating with each other," said Breindel.

Gittel stamped her foot. "What are they saying?"

Yossi opened his palm and stared at it.

"Show us! Show us!" cried the boys.

Without warning, Yossi called out, "Catch, Feivish!" He threw his stone high into the air and toward his brother.

Feivish caught it and looked at it. Then he yelled, "Yossi! Catch mine — don't let the water boy get it!"

"You saw that?"

Feivish threw his stone. Yossi caught it, inspected it, and the brothers laughed.

Their laughter became boisterous.

"It's so good to laugh..." said Yossi.

"...after three terrible days," said Feivish, finishing his brother's thought. He winked, and Yossi nodded. "One, two, three...*go*!"

They pitched the stones with all their might into the woods bordering the backyard. Zelig and Mottel raced one another to find the stones — a hopeless task.

Feivish and Yossi, laughing so hard they held their stomachs, collapsed onto the ground.

"For Heaven's sake!" Breindel said. "Come to your senses and tell us who selected the alef."

"Get up, you two sillies, and explain," said Gittel.

With their wives standing over them, Feivish and Yossi pulled themselves upright. They giggled and hiccuped like schoolboys — and looked like schoolboys. Decaying leaves stuck to their coats, and mud streaked their shirts and pants. Zelig and Mottel, having given up the search, gaped at their fathers.

"The message is clear, wouldn't you say, Yossi?"

"Clear as the noses on our faces!"

"And what would your clear noses be saying?" Breindel asked.

"The Ribbono shel Olam has other plans for us," Feivish replied. "*I* believe He is suggesting both of us learn together the way we always have..."

"...and both of us work until we have the money to buy goats and chickens," Yossi continued. "Meanwhile, we'll rise earlier to learn..."

"...and extend our nighttime learning hours," concluded Feivish.

Breindel nodded. "Your days will be longer. It may be a struggle, but with Hashem's help we'll succeed. I've been mending simple things for our neighbors. I've earned three kopecks."

"Really, Breindel?" Gittel said. "Perhaps I'll begin embroidering for them. More kopecks!"

"Yossi, what do you think of a little business in the marketplace?" Feivish said. "We can keep goats, geese, hens, horses, donkeys, and ducks from blocking the square. Animals do seem to like...us."

He paced with his hands folded behind him. "You could build, set up, and take down the pens, and I'll tend to the creatures. We'll save enough money, little by little, to buy ourselves two goats and four chickens — no, *four* goats and *eight* chickens!"

Yossi paced alongside his brother. He shrugged. "Sixteen chickens would be so bad? Eight goats so terrible?"

"We can buy an elephant!" said Zelig, hopping up and down.

"I want a monkey!" Mottel declared, slapping his hands together.

"We had only two goats and four chickens," Gittel said quietly, "but we were happy. It was because we had two men bringing Torah into our homes."

The laughter stopped.

"Gittel is wise," Breindel said.

Gittel's eyes shone as she smiled at her sister.

"Your wife is right," said Feivish. "The goal is to learn the way we did before — not to acquire a farm."

"Or a circus," Yossi added. "Feivish!" he said. "Look at the time. We must get to the *beis midrash* immediately!"

The two men thanked their wives, kissed the boys, and walked arm in arm to the *beis midrash*.

On the way, Yossi said, "Feivish, what a catch. Miraculous!"

"It was your incredible throw, Yossi! And you caught my stone as if I'd handed it to you. How far into the woods do you suppose they landed?"

"They never landed. The clouds caught them!"

"So, tell me, Yossele. How did you do it?"

"Do what?"

"Your stone. How did you get rid of it?"

"We threw them into the woods, Feivish..."

"Come on. How did you switch your alef for a blank?"

Yossi stopped. "I did not have an alef. You had it, and switched it for a blank. That's why I laughed..."

Feivish blinked.

"Feivish...you did switch your alef for a blank, didn't you?"

"No, I didn't," the older twin said slowly. "My stone was clean. I laughed because I thought *you* had made the switch."

"Well, if you didn't have the alef, and I didn't have it...where was it? The boys didn't come near it, and we all watched Gittel..."

The look-alikes gawked at one other, wordless, for a long, long moment.

"There was no alef stone," they said softly, in unison.

"But...what does that mean?"

"Do you think...?"

They whispered these questions and looked up to the Heavens in wonder and fear.

No alef stone.

Shaky, holding on to each other for support, the brothers made their way to the *beis midrash*. Once they had davened *minchah* and settled down, which took some time, they learned with more devotion and fire than they had ever before.

Their joy of learning Torah — together! — inspired everyone in the *beis midrash*.

CHAPTER TWELVE

A Chanukah Miracle

Breindel, Gittel, and the boys demand-
ed, begged, and teased to find out
which twin had drawn the alef. But
the men held on to their secret, promising to
reveal the outcome at the right time.

Chanukah began two nights later. In their
side-by-side ramshackle houses, Feivish

lit candles, and Yossi lit wicks that floated in olive oil. Two beautiful silver menorahs shone in their windowsills, reflecting the glow of golden flames.

The families celebrated together with dreidels, Chanukah gelt, raisins and nuts, and, of course, latkes. On the first night they feasted in Feivish's home. On the second, they would gather in Yossi's, and so it would go, back and forth, for all eight days.

Breindel and Gittel, warm and flushed from cooking and frying, served dishes of hot latkes, latkes, and more latkes, with applesauce they'd squirreled away for a treat. When no one could eat even one more little latke, Feivish and Yossi wiped their lips and leaned back in their chairs.

"Now," said Breindel. "We have been patient long enough. Tell us what happened with the lottery — what Hashem decided. Because surely He was in charge."

"You're right, sister-in-law," Yossi said. His voice shook just a little. "Hashem ran the

lottery. Feivish, tell them. You are the elder."

"No, Yossi. You."

Yossi smiled. He began with the first lottery, and ended with the brothers throwing their stones into the woods.

"Well, we *know* all that!" Breindel exclaimed. "What about the *stones*?"

"Who drew the alef?" Gittel asked.

The twin brothers looked at each other.

"There was no alef," they said quietly, one after the other.

After a moment of silent surprise, Gittel said, "What does that mean? Did you lose that stone? *I* didn't lose it, so don't blame..."

"No, no. No one lost anything, dear wife," said Yossi.

Feivish cleared his throat. "The last two stones were blank. Both of us saw both stones."

"Tatty, is this a trick?" asked Mottel.

Yossi untied a small sack hanging from a rope belt around his waist. "We found them in the field, not far from each other, so clean,

they almost shone. We thought we might have been mistaken, that one was indeed marked with an alef." He placed them on the table. Both were blank.

Breindel picked up the stones carefully. "I scrubbed them all with lye and a brush. Yes, I cleaned sixty stones; these look like the rest." She turned to Gittel. "Where are the rest of the stones?"

"I gathered them," Gittel said. "Now where did I put them... Hashem help me... Ah!" She picked up a rusted pail that sat under Breindel's sink. "They're in here."

Zelig and Mottel quickly inspected them. "No alefs. None."

"This is truly..." Feivish began.

"...miraculous," Yossi finished.

"Ah-*choo*, ah-*choo*, ah-*choo*, ah-*choo*, ah-*choo*!"

Gittel picked up the last two stones. "It's as if Hashem has washed one of them clean!"

All sat at the table examining the stones, stunned.

"Ah-*choo*, ah-*choo*, ah-*choo*, ah-*choo*, ah-*choo*!"

"Ah. Miraculous." Gittel looked to her husband. "Yossi, may I?" He nodded with a smile. "Yes. I will share my miracle. With Hashem's help, Mottel will have a baby brother or sister...in five months."

"Ah-*choo*, ah-*choo*, ah-*choo*, ah-*choo*, ah-*choo*!"

"Breindel! This is what you say about my miracle?"

"No!" Breindel cried, swiping at her nose with her apron. "In its proper time, Gittel, dear. And we..." She looked at Feivish, who ducked his head and nodded. "With Hashem's help, *we* will have a baby as well. A month after yours!"

Yossi slapped his leg. "Finally! We'll be older!"

The red-haired look-alikes grabbed their sons' hands, and the four of them sang and danced as the sisters clapped.

After the singing and dancing and plenty

of "in its proper time's," Breindel became unusually quiet.

"Dear wife?" Feivish was anxious. "Are you feeling all right?"

"Mama? Did you eat too many latkes?"

Gittel squinted. "What's the matter, Breindel?"

Tears bubbled in Breindel's eyes. "I sneezed. Five times. Then another five. And a third time. No one blessed me."

In unison, Feivish, Yossi, Zelig, Mottel, and Gittel blessed Breindel with a joyous "Gesundheit! Gesundheit! Gesundheit!"

Breindel added, "To all of us!"

The families turned to the window to see the menorah flames in Yossi's house suddenly burn brighter. And all the while, the menorah in Feivish's house bathed the families in marvelous, miraculous Chanukah light.

Glossary

am ha'aretz: uneducated person

bulvan: blockhead

deverkhen: wake up

essen: eat

gaon: genius

Gott in Himmel: God in Heaven

kloppers: man who would bang on windows in the shtetl to wake Jewish men for morning prayers

mensch (pl. menschen): person(s) of fine character

mishegas: craziness

Ribbono shel Olam: Master of the Universe

shlemiel: fool

shtetl: Jewish village in Europe and Russia

tipish: fool

vantz: bedbug

Acknowledgments

Many thanks to:

My rabbi, Rabbi Mordechai Swiatycki of Monsey, New York, whom I could never, ever thank sufficiently.

The One G-d for His endless gifts, including the privilege of seeing my work published.

About the Author

Andrea Ramon (aka Chana Rochel) Eller writes from a little neighborhood in Yerushalayim where she and her husband live. A member of the Society of Children's Book Writers and Illustrators and The Authors Guild, she is a musician with a degree in composition and arranging.

Andrea's writing, appearing in magazines and newspapers, includes feature stories and fiction. She now devotes her time to writing books for children aged five through thirteen.

More historical fiction for kids from Menucha!

LAIBEL'S LIBEL

M.C. MILLMAN

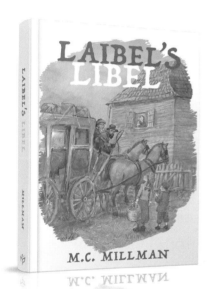

"*I just have this feeling, Laibel. I don't know why, but I'm scared.*"

"*Nothing is going to happen, Sarah. We live in modern times. It's 1849, and I'm the wealthiest man in Luxembourg. No one would dare harm us.*"

When Laibel Landsman is falsely accused of a terrible crime and thrown into jail, the entire Jewish community fears for its safety. Laibel's children and friends mount a desperate search to prove his innocence before it's too late.

MENUCHA PUBLISHERS

Available wherever Jewish books are sold or at www.menuchapublishers.com